FIRESTORMERS

Firestormers is published by
Stone Arch Books,
a Capstone imprint
1710 Roe Crest Drive
North Mankato, Minnesota 56003
www.mycapstone.com

Cataloging-in-Publication Data is available on the
Library of Congress website.
ISBN: 978-1-4965-3305-0 (library binding)
ISBN: 978-1-4965-3309-8 (eBook)

Summary:
While training new members for the FIRESTORMERS,
the world's newest, most elite wildfire fighting crew, a
group of recruits goes missing inside a massive blaze.
Their trainer, former special operations soldier Heath
Rodgers, blames himself for their mistakes. If the new
recruits are going to survive, Rodgers must lead the
Firestormers into the flames before the past comes back
to burn him.

Printed and bound in Canada.
009638F16

FIRESTORMERS
BACK BURN

written by CARL BOWEN
cover illustration by MARC LEE

STONE ARCH BOOKS
a capstone imprint

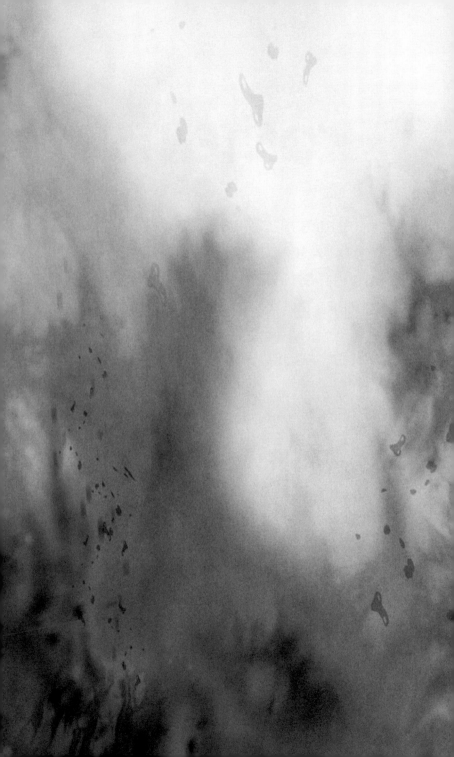

CONTENTS

FIRESTORMERS
Elite Firefighting Crew

As the climate changes and the population grows, wildland fires increase in number, size, and severity. Only an elite group of men and women are equipped to take on these immense infernos. Like the toughest military units, they have the courage, the heart, and the technology to stand on the front lines against hundred-foot walls of 2,000-degree flames. They are the FIRESTORMERS.

NORTH CASCADES NATIONAL PARK

Established:

October 2, 1968

Coordinates:

48°49′58″ N

121°20′51″ W

Location:

Washington, USA

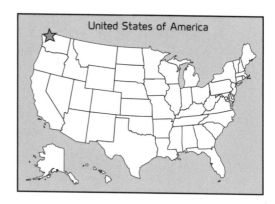

United States of America

Size:

504,781 acres (789 square miles)

Elevation Range:

605–9,206 feet above sea level

Ecology:

Jagged mountain peaks tower over the landscape of North Cascades National Park, the third largest National Park in North America. Douglas fir, western hemlock, and Pacific silver fir line the foothills, along with hundreds of other plant species. Bald eagles, wolves, grizzly bears, and mountain lions call these forests home.

MAP

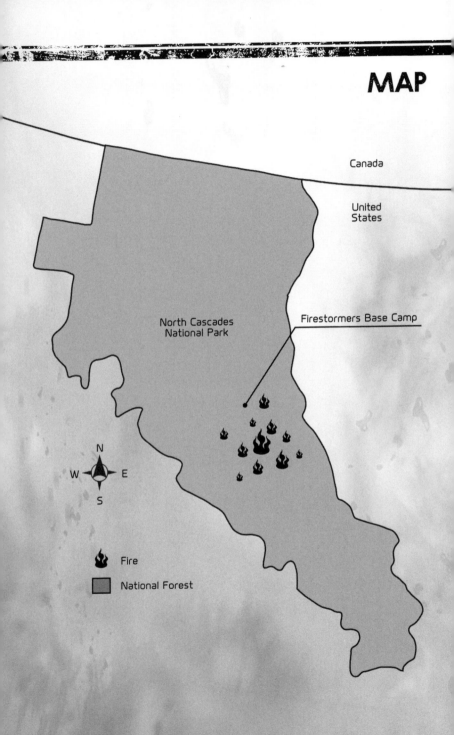

Canada

United States

North Cascades National Park

Firestormers Base Camp

N
W E
S

🔥 Fire

⬛ National Forest

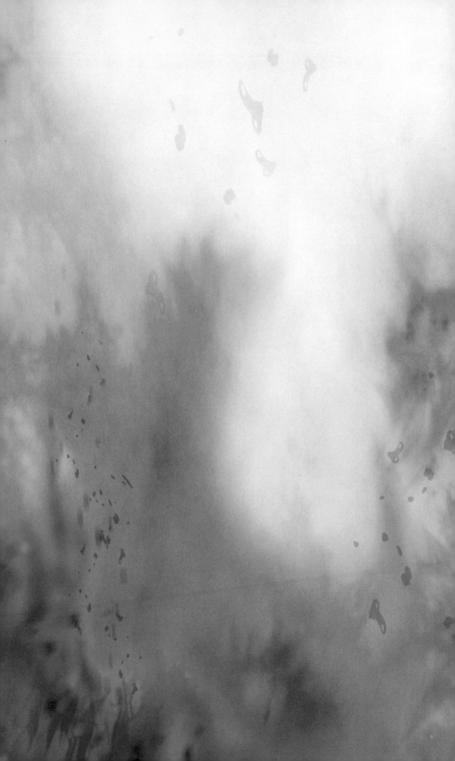

CHAPTER ONE

The air hung hot and heavy in North Cascades National Park. Just breathing in the thick air was miserable, and the early morning sun had just peeked through the trees.

Not that the sun would be a concern. A blotchy black and gray smear stained the sky for miles in every direction, leaching light and color. On a better day, that gray overcast would have indicated an oncoming storm. But today, it signaled the opposite. The gray mass wasn't a cloud, but smoke, pouring upward from the ever-growing wildfire.

The wildfire had been burning for almost a week, and it wasn't the only such fire in the state. Local fire services were overwhelmed and running themselves ragged, just as they had been since before the beginning of the official fire season. So rather than pulling resources from another fire that couldn't spare them, the locals had appealed to the federal government for help.

That help had finally come, in the form of a new, high-tech firefighting force, funded by the U.S. Forest Service.

That force was officially titled the National Elite Interagency Wildfire Rapid Response Strike Force. Its members called themselves the Firestormers.

Their job was to show up on the scene of a wildland fire incident, take over command for the local fire services, coordinate all efforts, and lead the way in the field.

The Firestormers employed the best firefighters from all over the country and equipped them with top-of-the-line gear. They attacked the front lines to contain and control fires as quickly as humanly possible. They worked long hours for days, often weeks, at a time, racing from one wildfire to the next with precious little downtime between.

Wherever, whenever the Firestormers were needed, there they would be.

Today, they were needed in Washington State. As the sun came up behind its smoke-hidden horizon, the leader of the Firestormers' premier strike team gathered his team members for their first briefing.

The effort's staging area was a shopping mall parking lot that was still under construction. This section of the lot was packed with fire engines, water tenders, buggies, bulldozers, and other heavy equipment.

The strike team's leader, Lieutenant Jason Garrett, had set up a folding screen behind one of his crew's buggies. He stood beside it with a tablet computer datapad. The datapad connected wirelessly to a pocket-sized projector. With a tap on his datapad, Garrett brought the projector to life, displaying an image of the green and yellow U.S. Forest Service shield logo.

Sergeant Heath Rodgers stood up in the front rank of the lieutenant's audience. He was the boss of one of the four-hand hand crews that made up the strike force. Like himself, every member of Rodgers's team was ex-military. Also like himself, every member of his crew had more wildland firefighting experience than their young lieutenant.

Rodgers had been leading a Hotshot crew with a local unit since before Garrett had graduated college, and that was after

Rodgers had spent more than a dozen years in the Marine Corps. Because of his age and experience, Rodgers should have been chosen to lead this strike team.

Garrett's father was a U.S. Senator, however, and the lieutenant had been a sort of local celebrity back home in Oregon. Apparently, those sorts of connections counted a bit more than age and experience.

It's hardly the first time I've been passed over for a promotion, Rodgers thought. It wasn't the first time he'd had that thought either.

"All right, I guess let's recap," Garrett began. "The locals are calling this the Thunder Creek Complex. It started a week ago. Or, rather, that's when somebody got far enough out into the wilderness to notice the smoke. Weather reporting suggests there was heavy lightning activity at that time. It was hot and dry, so that's our likely cause."

Sergeant Rodgers took a deep, patient breath and tried not to sigh. He'd sat through plenty of Garrett's stumbling, plodding briefings, but they never got easier to endure.

"Anyway," the lieutenant continued, his eyes glued to his tablet datapad, "local fire services reported eight separate smoke sightings on that first day. The sightings spread out across the Thunder Creek region as you see here." Garrett nodded toward the folding screen.

"It's a little out of focus, Lieutenant," Rodgers said.

At that, Garrett looked up to see the Forest Service logo projected on the screen. His ears turned a shade of pink. "Oops. Forgot to connect the . . . Yeah, here it is."

He tapped on his tablet and swiped what was on it toward the projector hanging above the screen. The logo disappeared, to be replaced by a satellite photo of the Thunder Creek area. Rodgers remembered it fondly. He'd grown up nearby and been out there camping, hiking, and hunting many times. This photo had obviously been taken at some time before the start of the fire.

"Okay," Garrett was saying, still tapping away on his tablet, "now the overlay . . ."

At his command, a contour map of the same area appeared and lined up over it, showing changes in elevation across the area. One more command caused eight labeled points to appear in the more thickly forested sections of the map.

"There we go," Garrett said, checking the screen against what his tablet computer said. He looked out at his strike team and grinned sheepishly. "Sheesh. Technology minus coffee equals comedy, am I right?"

Most of the Firestormers chuckled.

Sergeant Rodgers didn't. This briefing would be over now if he'd been running it.

"So, as I was saying before I so rudely interrupted myself," Garrett went on, "these are our ignition sources. Before local services could deploy, a high wind from the north pushed our three northernmost fires together."

Garrett advanced the projection to later in the time line. The ignition points on the map were now surrounded by larger red fields outlining the fires' spread. As he said, the three highest fire areas on the map had grown together into one larger mass. The rest of the smaller fires were still separate, but even at this stage, they were in dangerously close together.

"At the end of day two," Garrett said, "a shift in wind spread this northern fire over the locals' fire lines and pushed it east, where it joined up with these two fires."

He advanced the projection again to illustrate his point. On the map, the top five most northern ignition points were surrounded by one long irregular area that was all on fire.

"The other three fires were still isolated, but you can see the progression here," the lieutenant continued. "The southwestern fire is already spreading in the same direction as the main mass, though it hadn't yet linked up at that point. The remaining two fires had grown together as well."

As he mentioned each point, Garrett tapped his tablet. The isolated fire fields below the main mass lit up on the projection screen as he indicated them.

"A little bit of good news by Friday," Garrett said, advancing the projection ahead again. It focused on the smaller section of the fire complex that centered on the three ignition sources in the southeastern corner of the Thunder Creek area. The fire area indicated on the map was slightly larger than it had been in the previous overlay, but it was now surrounded on three sides by an unbroken black line.

"Favorable winds and a rise in humidity kept this lower southeastern fire from spreading too quickly," he said. "Locals have achieved almost one hundred percent containment on it. If all goes well, it shouldn't pose any risk of slipping their lines and joining up with the main body."

Garrett sighed and advanced the projection once more to show the entire complex area again. The contained fire remained on the lower right, but now an ugly red smear with only a few broken black lines around it marred the entire top half of the map.

"But, for those of you who like your good

news seasoned with plenty of bad, locals weren't able to get a hold of this last fire from the southwest. As the main mass has grown, it's spread down to this smaller fire and combined forces. This, ladies and gents, is what we're up against."

Rodgers narrowed his eyes and examined the fire area. It appeared to be spreading north and east along the topography of the land, following Thunder Creek. That area was all foothills and forest and shrubbery, with one or two scenic-drive highways cutting through them. A few lazy rivers doodled crooked lines through the area as well.

Rodgers had fished in those waters. Now, on the screen, the spreading fire looked like the claw of some imponderable beast clutching greedily at the land.

"All right," Garrett continued, "this fire's spreading slowly now — for a fire anyway

— so we don't have an army backing us up. There's us and a few hundred more locals to spread out all around the perimeter. The chief's deploying them to the north and west to finish up the lines they've already started."

Division Chief Anna MacElreath was the head of the Firestormers organization. Answering directly to the Forest Service, she took over as the incident commander whenever her people were assigned to a fire like this and passed orders down through her staff to all the firefighters in the field. Today she was running the show from an incident command post set up at a fire station just outside North Cascades National Park.

"That means we get the fun job," Garrett went on. "Chief needs us to get in here under this main mass on the eastern half and keep the fire from spreading down to the isolated fire the locals have almost contained."

"Any idea who's working the isolated fire?" Rodgers asked, frowning at the incomplete fire lines around the smaller fire.

Garrett looked up blinking his eyes. "Huh? Um, I'm not . . ." He tapped his tablet a few times and scratched his head. "No, it doesn't say here. Why?"

Sergeant Rodgers considered telling him the truth, but he didn't really see how it was relevant to the briefing. Nor did he consider it any of Garrett's business. Instead, he said, "If we're going to be watching their backs, we should know if we can rely on them to be watching ours."

Lieutenant Garrett looked at him for a moment then gave him a small frustrated frown. "Well, judging by the terrain it'll have to be a Hotshot crew. The fire's too far off the roads for dozers, engines or tenders. They're locals so they know the area. They managed eighty percent containment in just a few days, so they're obviously good. Add that to the fact that the chief let them stay where they are after she decided where to send us. I guess if you trust the chief's judgment, you can safely assume this Hotshot crew's going to be just fine watching your back. Any more questions?"

Garrett's tone suggested he would prefer an answer in the negative. Rodgers gave him one.

"Okay, so let's talk strategy," Garrett said. "As I mentioned, this terrain's too tough for vehicles. Roads running through the area are closed, and none of them lead where we need to go anyway. There's no good landing zones for a smokejump either, so we're Hotshotting on this one."

Half of the Firestormers looked disappointed and the rest seemed relieved.

Those who had been smokejumpers before becoming Firestormers would have preferred to do things their usual way — namely to fly over the fire in a small plane and parachute out in front of it with all their gear so they could set up and get to work. Those who'd been Hotshots, however, saw no problem with driving out as close to the fire as they could on surface streets and then hiking in overland to set up camp and get to work. Both sorts of crews did the same sort of work once they got to the fire. It was really only their means of getting there that differed.

Rodgers had been a Hotshot himself, but he actually preferred the smokejumper method. He'd done plenty of parachuting during his tours in the Marines, and into places much more dangerous than any wildfire line. Joining the Firestormers had allowed everyone to cross -rain in smokejumping and

Hotshotting, and Rodgers had found it one of the most exhilarating aspects of the work. That Garrett clearly found it terrifying and was only too glad to avoid it whenever he could was yet one more reason for Rodgers to resent the young lieutenant's rise to his position of authority.

"We'll drive out on this road," Garrett was saying, highlighting the asphalt artery on the screen. "There's an RV park . . . here. We'll park the buggies and set up camp there. Park's closed, for obvious reasons, so we should have the place to ourselves."

"There's another campsite about a mile closer to where we need to be," Rodgers pointed out.

"I see it," Garrett said. "I considered it, but it's deeper between the two fires. If one or the other blows up in the night, I don't want us caught between the hammer and the anvil, if you know what I'm saying."

Rodgers let that go with a nod, and the briefing went on. And on . . . and on. Rodgers was used to it. The last guy he'd served under in the military had been just as much a fan giving long-winded briefings.

CHAPTER TWO

A short while later, the Firestormers were loaded up in two buggies and were trundling down the deserted road toward Thunder Creek. The buggies were fifteen-passenger, two-wheel-drive buses painted white with the Firestormer logo stenciled on one side and the Forest Service shield on the other.

Each buggy held twelve Firestormers, and the back section was caged off and contained the crews' gear. The vehicles were only minutes away from the fire front. Rodgers was sitting in the rear seat over the wheel well. Sharing it with him was Sergeant Amalia Rendon, one of his fellow crew bosses. Rendon was from New Mexico and had been a TV journalist before joining her local fire service. She reminded Rodgers of some of the women he'd served with in the military — tough, disciplined and every bit as capable as the men, whether those men wanted to admit it or not. Rodgers admired thos qualities.

"That guy's a major problem," Sergeant Rodgers mumbled under his breath.

Rodgers had been staring out the window for most of the trip, lost in his own thoughts. Sergeant Rendon had been amusing herself making conversation with the other firefighters around her, which suited Rodgers just fine. Now, it seemed it was his turn.

"What guy are you talking about?" Sergeant Rendon asked Rodgers. "The lieutenant?"

"If you want to call him that," Rodgers replied.

"You're not still bitter that MacElreath chose him instead of you?"

Rodgers scoffed. "It's hardly the first time I've been passed over for a promotion." *Although this time did sting the most,* he thought.

"Then what are you griping about?" Rendon pressed. "You really want to be stuck back at camp, handling paperwork and arguing with the chief? You're a grunt like me. You want to slash your way through this beast and help out the local departments like a hero. Am I right?"

"Speaking of the local departments," Rendon began, "why did you really ask Garrett who the Hotshots were working those isolated fires?"

Sergeant Rodgers looked up at the sky. "Curiosity, I guess."

"Oh, wow," Rendon replied, smirking. "We've really got to play poker sometime."

Rodgers grinned a little at that.

"Seriously, though," Sergeant Rendon said. "The Lieutenant let it drop, but I know you better than he does."

"You both met me the same day in training," Rodgers pointed out.

"Sure, but you don't go out of your way to second-guess me in front of everybody, and you don't seem to think I don't belong here. If you did, I wouldn't pay you much attention either."

"Fair point," Rodgers muttered.

"So — and don't change the subject this time — what's up? Why the interest?"

Rodgers took a deep breath, considering not telling her. It wasn't her business any more than it was Garrett's. Still, he liked Rendon. He respected her. She was friendly and personable without letting it affect her professionalism. Plus, it wasn't like it was any big secret.

"I'm from here," he said, pulling the steel machete from his utility belt. "Not Thunder Creek specifically, but not too far away. We used to come out here to hunt and fish and camp and that. My family and I did, that is."

"Do they still live out here?"

Sergeant Rodgers tapped nervously on the window. "Here and there. They spread out a little when my parents retired."

"Are they military, like you?" Rendon asked tentatively.

Rodgers shook his head. "I'm the only one who went in for that. The rest of them are all in the fire service. It wasn't until my last hitch ended that I joined the family business."

"Ah, I see," Sergeant Rendon said. "So

you think some of them might be out here working this fire. Yeah?"

"Just one," Rodgers said. "My folks and my uncles are all retired out. My oldest brother's a fire marshal in San Diego, and the next one down works in Seattle. But my youngest brother, Ethan . . . he's a Hotshot with a company up north here. This fire's in their jurisdiction."

"Does Lieutenant Garrett know about this?"

"Doubt it. I never brought it up."

"It might be a good way to find out what you were asking about," Rendon pointed out.

"Doesn't matter," Sergeant Rodgers said. "I was just curious anyway. It's nothing worth bringing to Garrett's attention."

"Barring that," Rendon suggested, "you could always just call your brother. You know, if doing things the easy way doesn't gall you too much."

Rodgers shrugged uncomfortably and grunted.

Sergeant Rendon chuckled. "Slow down there, Shakespeare. You want to put that in modern English for me?"

"It's not that big a deal," Rodgers said.

"So you're not going to call him or ask Garrett to find out if he's out here?"

"Nope."

"Why not?" asked Rendon.

Rodgers tapped the window a few more times. "Ethan doesn't want to talk to me anyway."

"Why not?"

Rodgers sighed. "Because I don't feel like answering all of his personal questions whenever he starts prying into my business. Like you are."

Rendon huffed in frustration but didn't seem too offended by Rodgers shutting her down. She elbowed him again and said, "You're no fun."

Rodgers gave her a faint grin. "Don't pout."

At that, the buggy stopped. Sergeant Rodgers and his crew hopped out, leaving Rendon and her crew behind to head to the next fire line.

As the buggies left them, Sergeant Rodgers looked up at the gray sky again, and he thought about the last time he and his brother had spoken.

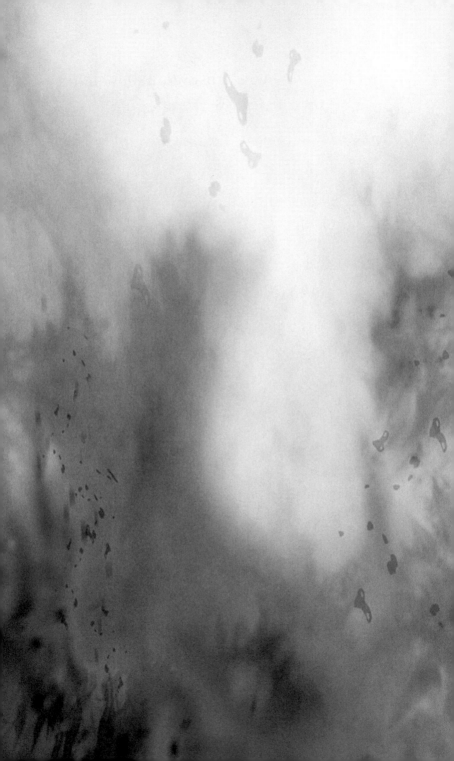

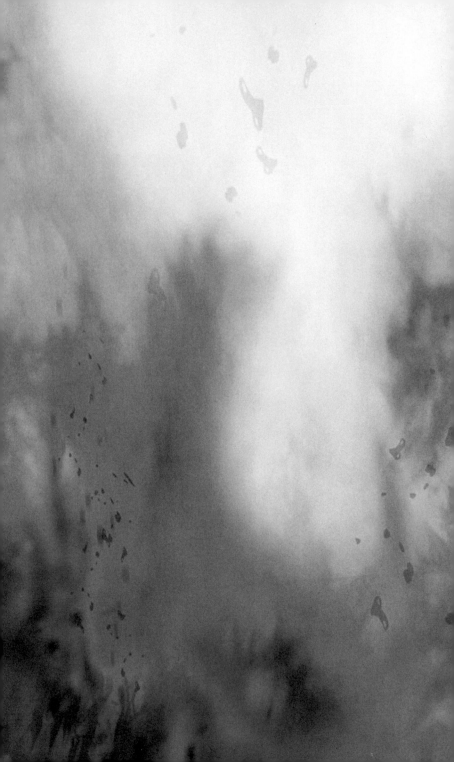

CHAPTER THREE

The problems began Thanksgiving of the previous year. The family had all piled into the home of Rodgers's eldest brother, Ian, to devour a fourteen-pound turkey and digest it over the course of several football games. The second game was just starting, but Rodgers had excused himself to the porch for a little peace and quiet. A big meal made him sleepy, but between his older brother William's kids, Ian's dogs, and the close quarters of Ian's living room, restful peace was in short supply.

Once outside, Rodgers plopped down in

one of Ian's rocking chairs and stared out at the carpet of leaves that Ian called a front yard. Tufts of brown grass poked up through the leaves. Ian wasn't much for yard work.

Rodgers's peaceful meditation lasted all of five minutes.

"Well here's where you're hiding," Ethan said, letting the screen door bang behind him. He stomped onto the porch in his big steel-toe logging boots, zipping up a bomber jacket that used to belong to their father. He held a huge, Sherlock Holmes-style pipe. "Mind if I join you?"

"You're smoking now?" Rodgers asked him.

Ethan sat down on the porch rail and gestured toward Rodgers with the pipe. "Want to try it?"

"I'd rather live, thanks."

"Suit yourself," Ethan said with a shrug.

"You don't know what you're missing." He took a deep breath in through his nose, stuck the stem of the pipe in his mouth, and blew through it. A steady stream of bright bubbles rose out of it and danced in the chilly November breeze.

Rodgers laughed despite himself. "You idiot."

Ethan smiled wider than the porch. "I got you. It's good to see you laughing again. You haven't done that much since you got back."

Rodgers shrugged.

"So how are you doing with . . ." Ethan gestured vaguely with the pipe, " . . . all that?"

"It's getting better," Rodgers said. "The guys at the VA hospital are helping out. Everything's pretty much okay."

"Good, good." Ethan paused, unsure what to add. "Glad to hear it. That's good."

Silence settled. Rodgers found it funny

sometimes the way people tried to talk to him about his time in the military. No one seemed to know how to do it. At best, they talked around it. Most were only too happy to change the subject.

"So who are they watching for halftime in there?" he asked. The topic shift untied a knot of tension in his little brother's shoulders.

"Redskins, if you can believe it. As soon as halftime's over, they're going back to the Cowboys."

Ethan paused for a bit. He blew another stream of bubbles from his pipe, grinned at himself again, and then set the toy aside. Rodgers could tell he wanted to talk about something. Heath rocked back and closed his eyes, letting Ethan work his courage up.

"So, I've been reading about your program," he said at last.

"With the VA?"

"No, the Forest Service one. The Firestormers. I've been reading about you guys. You'll be doing good work. Mind if I ask you some questions about it?"

Heath shrugged but didn't open his eyes. "Sure."

"How'd you get involved? Did you . . . like . . . apply? Were you recruited? Is there some kind of list?"

Rodgers grinned to himself. "You wouldn't believe me if I told you."

"Come on, man."

"The former Secretary of State recommended me to the chief in charge of the program."

"What? Bull," said his brother.

Rodgers chuckled. "Why you asking, kiddo? You writing my biography or something?"

"No, I'm serious," Ethan insisted. "I want to know. I want to join."

Rodgers opened one eye to find his little brother staring at him. "For real?"

"Yeah, man. So do I have to apply, or . . . What?"

Rodgers sat forward in his chair and gave Ethan his best serious-older-brother stare — one the pair of them had seen plenty of times from Ian and William when they were kids.

"You don't want to do that," he said quietly.

"Why not? It can't be all that different from what I'm already doing."

"Exactly," Rodgers said. "You're a Hotshot, and doing a fine job at it. Being a Firestormer's just harder work for not much better pay."

"'A fine job'?" Ethan replied. "I'm actually a pretty great Hotshot, thank you. I just made crew boss last month. That's faster than you did it."

"So why are you in such a hurry to leave?"

"Because being a Firestormer's just . . . I

don't know. Better. You guys are the elite. The elite of the elite. You said so yourself."

"It's not what it's cracked up to be."

"The heck it isn't," Ethan snapped. "You're still in it. What's your problem with me wanting to be in it too? I'm not asking for a recommendation. I just want to know if I can fill out a dang application."

"I don't think it would suit you," Rodgers said, as nicely as possible, which wasn't very. "The on-call hours are a nightmare, and there's constant traveling during the fire season. Plus, right now there's no opportunity for promotion."

"Oh, this is such a load," Ethan barked, turning away once more. "Wouldn't suit me? What does that even mean? You don't think I can handle it?"

Rodgers paused to try to figure out how to phrase what he was thinking.

The pause proved to be just a bit too long.

"You don't!" Ethan said when Rodgers didn't respond right away. "Oh, that's nice. You know, I've been a firefighter longer than you have, Heath. If you think you're so much better than me —"

"Boys," a voice called from behind the screen door. Rodgers and Ethan glanced over to see their mother standing inside, looking out at them. "Everything okay out here?"

"Yes, ma'am," they said together.

"The game's back on. Don't sit out here in the cold too long."

"Yes, ma'am," they said again.

Their mother nodded and shut the inner door. Rodgers and Ethan sat scowling in different directions a while longer. When no more words came from either of them, Ethan gave it up and pulled the screen door open.

"Wait, Ethan," Rodgers said, heaving a

sigh. "There's an application process, and we are currently recruiting. Download the forms, get your lieutenant to sign them, and mail them to the address on our website. There's a written test, a couple of interviews, a background check, and a PT test. If you want to be a Firestormer, those are the hoops you've got to jump through. I can't do anything to help you out, though."

"I wouldn't expect you to," Ethan said. He looked down, a bitterly disappointed frown on his face. Then he went back inside in a huff.

CHAPTER FOUR

Sergeant Rodgers loved the first day on a big fire. He reveled in it. His bullnecked, all-veteran crew was at the head of today's fire line. That meant they constantly bumped into uncut territory and hiked through the toughest forests.

Rodgers was an old hand at orienteering, and he had personal experience with these woods. Still, in an area the size of North Cascades, he would've been hopelessly lost without his lifeline back to Lieutenant Garrett, and without his ranger, Calvin Walker.

His lifeline was the tough smartphone-sized datapad secured in the Nomex bracer on the inside of his right forearm. On it, he checked maps and satellite imagery of the area in real time, and Lieutenant Garrett sent him information from up the Incident Command pipeline. The datapad also tracked him via GPS and kept Garrett informed of his location.

As invaluable as the datapads were, Rodgers actually found himself relying on his ranger more. Calvin Walker helped Rodgers's crew stay on course through the trackless forest or guide them around obstacles that would have cost them countless time backtracking.

Walker didn't stick around to chitchat when he checked in periodically — he didn't even eat his lunch with the crew. So it was surprising that he was nearby when Garrett checked in at midday.

Rodgers pressed the Accept button on the datapad. "Afternoon, Lieutenant. What's the matter . . . don't trust us to do our job out here?"

Rodgers smiled at Walker, and Walker smiled back hesitantly.

Lieutenant Garrett hemmed and hawed on the other end of the line.

"Get on with it, sir," Rodgers blurted out. "Some of us have work to do."

"There's a problem," Garrett admitted.

"Is something going on?" Rodgers asked, recognizing the seriousness in his voice.

"That team that was working the isolated fire to the south — remember them?" Garrett asked.

Yeah, of course I do, Rodgers thought.

"The Hotshots? They're missing."

"How the heck did that happen?"

"It started with radio trouble last night,"

Garrett explained. "They were breaking up all through the end of the day. Patchy signal. Garbled transmissions. Operations Section said they made an almost unintelligible transmission at the end of their shift when they were returning to base. They should have checked in this morning, but they haven't yet. They're completely silent, and their fire's starting to slip containment."

"That's a problem," Rodgers said. If the lower fire burned up to the main mass, it was going to catch the Firestormers from behind and Incident Command would have to redraw new containment lines around the whole area.

"That isn't all," Garrett said.

Rodgers's blood ran cold. His fingers numbed.

"Those Hotshots . . ." the lieutenant continued. "They're the Okanogan Badgers."

"That's my brother's company."

"I know," Lieutenant Garrett said. "Sergeant Rendon radioed me this morning and told me you had a brother working out here."

Of course she did, Rodgers thought.

"I just spoke with Chief MacElreath at Incident Command," continued the lieutenant. "She confirmed that the crew is missing."

"Well, what's being done?" Rodgers demanded. "Is search and rescue out yet?"

"They've got a helicopter coming."

Rodgers shook his head. "Over those woods, a helicopter's not going to be much help. They need people on the ground, searching the area. People who know the land."

"I know," Garrett said. "That's the plan. The helicopter's just a Band-Aid."

"And I need to be with them," Rodgers

said, not listening to Garrett. "I know this area pretty well, and I've done search and rescue before."

"I know," Garrett said.

"Look, he's my brother, Lieutenant," Rodgers said, his volume rising. "I'm doing this. I'll start walking from here if I have to."

"Whoa, take it easy, Heath," Garrett said. "I agree with you. In fact, search and rescue's coming to pick you up right now. That's what the helicopter's for. They're going to take you and Walker over to your brother's camp to start looking. In the meantime, I've split the rest of your crew up between Rendon and Richards."

Rodgers blinked a few times, too dumbstruck to react. He looked down at the thermos in his hand. Finally he said, "You already did all that?"

"As soon as they told me about your

brother," Garrett replied. "I just assumed you'd want to go help find him. That's what I would want to do."

"Thanks."

Lieutenant Garrett grunted. "Sure. Helicopter should be there in five minutes. Get what you need, and be ready to go."

"Will do," Walker chimed in for both of them.

Rodgers heard the lieutenant switch off his radio, and he did the same. Then he turned to Walker. "Ethan," Rodgers said quietly. "His name's Ethan. My baby brother."

Walker squeezed Rodgers's shoulder. "We'll find him."

"He'd be here right now if it weren't for me."

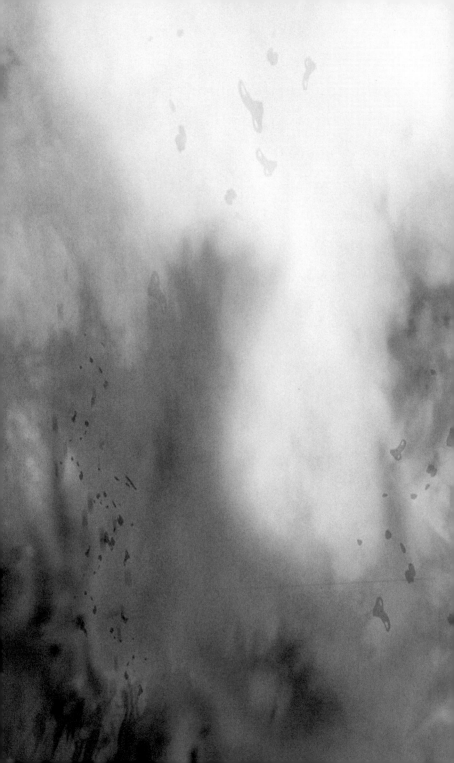

CHAPTER FIVE

A couple of weeks before fire season officially started, Chief MacElreath had called Rodgers into her office at the Firestormers' headquarters. Rodgers's first suspicion, irrational though it may have been, was that Lieutenant Garrett had already written him up for something stupid, and he was being called on the carpet for it. He took a seat across the oak desk from the chief and mentally prepared himself to deal with a hassle.

"Good lord, C-3PO, why don't you try to

relax?" Chief MacElreath said, grinning. "I've never seen anybody try to be at attention sitting down before. Take it easy. This isn't the principal's office."

Rodgers grinned despite himself and relaxed in his chair. Though he wasn't a fan of the chief's sense of humor, it had a certain charm. Her south Georgia accent lent it a disarming folksiness.

"So what can I do for you, Chief?"

"PT tests were yesterday for the potential recruits," Chief MacElreath said. "I'm having everybody who passed sit down with Garrett for some one-on-one interviews. After that, you and the other crew bosses can go over their files and cherry-pick which ones you want. Final say is up to Garrett, but I trust you four to work out any disagreements before you take your picks to him."

"I doubt that'll be a problem," Rodgers

said. "We know what we like in our crews."

"Good, good. Now, before any of that stuff happens, there was a matter I wanted to bring up with you personally first. You know your brother Ethan put in his application this round, yes?"

Rodgers nodded. His mom had mentioned it the last time he'd talked to her. Ethan hadn't had much to say to him since Thanksgiving.

"I had a good long chat with him during our interview," said the chief. "Seems like a good kid."

"He didn't bring up my name, did he?"

MacElreath shook her head. "I practically had to drag it out of him that you're his brother. You aren't even listed on his application. He's pretty concerned about the appearance of favoritism. He told me he didn't want any special consideration."

"That's good," Rodgers said, relieved.

"Frankly, though, he kind of needs it," Chief MacElreath went on. "Your brother's a good firefighter and all, don't get me wrong. There's not so much as a write-up for showing up late to work in his file. But for all there's nothing negative, there's nothing outstanding in there either. He just gets the job done, and that's pretty much it. The captains he's worked for were polite about it when I called them, but they all agree."

Rodgers frowned, unsure what the chief wanted from him. "How'd he do on the tests?"

MacElreath glanced at her computer. "Not bad. Solid B on the written. Passed the practical, but you've got to cut your own foot off to fail that part. He was borderline on the PT test. Did okay on the pack run, but his time was on the bad side of the curve.

Rodgers winced. "I'm not sure what I can say to that, Chief."

"Just tell me this," Chief MacElreath said. "The reason I called you in here is because I don't know your brother like you know him. He's pretty young. In my eyes, he's borderline, but he might have potential. You know him. Does he have what it takes — right now — to be one of us, or should I send him back to the minors to train up for a season?"

"Send him back," Rodgers shot back.

"You don't want to think about that a little?"

Rodgers shook his head. "I don't think he's ready."

"He's been fighting fires longer than you have," MacElreath pointed out.

"It wasn't just my firefighting experience that got me here," Rodgers said. "Ethan's never really sought out challenges. That's why he hasn't distinguished himself yet. Turning him down might help put that in perspective for him."

"It could light a fire under him, I suppose," Chief MacElreath said. She thought about it a moment, scratching idly at her wrist under the cuff of her sleeve. "All right, then. I'll cut him and have a chat with him about it."

"Sounds good," Rodgers said. "Is there anything else?"

"I appreciate your candor. I don't want you to go away feeling like you threw your brother under the bus. I needed your honest opinion."

"It's for his own good," Rodgers replied. "And the good of the team, of course."

"True, true."

Rodgers rose, said his goodbyes, and headed for the door. Before he could leave, Chief MacElreath called him back one last time.

"Hey, Heath? Your brother can always apply again next year. I'll make that clear to him."

"Yes, ma'am."

"And this program's always growing," Chief MacElreath added. "This time next year, if he makes the cut, you might just have a strike team of your own to put him on."

"Yes, ma'am," Heath said again. "Definitely something worth thinking about."

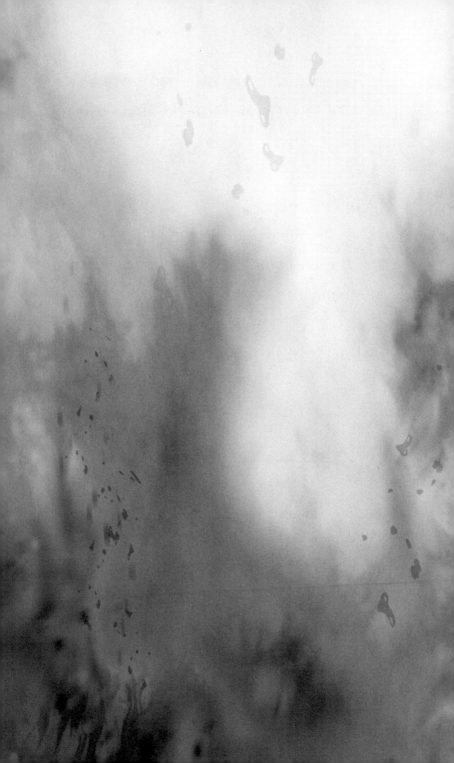

CHAPTER SIX

"Oh crud," muttered Rodgers, looking out of the window of the search-and-rescue chopper.

On the ground below, he saw that the isolated fire his brother was working was in danger of growing out of control. Already, the lower fire had begun to spread out from containment. Tendrils of flame spread out through the opening like a hand desperately clawing up out of a well. If the contained part of the fire were a seed, these tendrils were the shoots pushing out for sun and air. As they spread, a high wind rose in the south, whipping the flames up higher and pushing them out farther and faster. Time was running out to get this fire back under control.

All hope was not lost, however. Now that search and rescue was involved, it was just a matter of time before Sergeant Rodgers and the searchers found Ethan and his crew. If everyone was all right, Rodgers could reconnect them with Incident Command and get them back to work. In the meantime, the suppression effort still had one thing going for it: the Air Operations branch.

On a fire of this size, air operations were essential. In the early stages, light planes such as the Firestormers' CASA-212 delivered smokejumpers to remote regions of the fire. As the suppression effort developed, smaller cargo planes delivered supplies to those crews camping near the fire lines. Search-and-rescue operations and medical evacuation missions were handled by helicopter. More recently, tech specialists from the Incident Command staff had begun to employ quad-rotor and fixed-wing UAV drones to monitor fire conditions and keep up with suppression efforts.

Even more important was the role Air Operations played in the direct suppression effort. On fires like this one, a fleet of air tankers ran continuous missions over the burning land, carrying one thousand to twenty thousand gallons of fire retardants. When they were over the right area, they opened their tanks and spread their payloads like bombers dropping explosives.

Water was the preferred payload, as choppers could pump it into their tanks via hose from local sources or dunk and fill collapsible "Bambi buckets" suspended underneath. Some planes could even skim water right off the surface of a large enough body and drop payload after payload wherever they were needed.

Certain chemical retardants were in common use as well, especially early in the suppression effort. Combining select phosphates with thickeners, preservatives and other additives, the chemicals blanketed a target area with sticky, lumpy clumps that cut off the fire's oxygen and suffocated it. As the chemicals broke down, they acted as fertilizers to help the burnt land recover.

The planes and choppers that made up the Air Operations fleet were the property of the Forest Service for wildfire suppression. Their activities were coordinated from Incident Command, under the umbrella of Operations Section. In sweeping coordinated flights, the tankers either swarmed isolated fires or flew along the fire lines to supplement ground efforts.

Sergeant Rodgers was normally too busy to even think about ongoing air operations, but today he had a good perspective on the entire aerial mission. For as far as the eye could see, Forest Service tankers and helicopters dipped in and out of the smoke and over the flames like a swarm of bees. Thinking about the organization that kept them all out of each other's way made his job of hiking long miles and digging ditches seem like child's play.

I'll leave that headache to Garrett, he thought.

An alert on Rodgers's datapad beeped, drawing his attention back toward the ground. Walker's smart watch beeped at the same time.

"This is the place," Walker said, checking his watch against the readout on the projector lens built onto his smart goggles. "I think."

They had arrived at the site where Operations Section Chief Michael Farrant said Ethan and company had built their camp. Rodgers wore a frown to match the uncertainty in Walker's voice. He tapped the helicopter pilot on the shoulder and signaled him to take a lap around the area. The pilot nodded and banked the aircraft into a long, slow turn.

"It's burned," Rodgers said. Below them, the ground was black and smoldering with gnarly skeletal fingers of burnt tree trunks sticking out irregularly. *A complete boneyard,* Rodgers thought.

Some two hundred yards away lay the break in the Okanogan Badgers' fire line. A strategic air tanker bombardment had temporarily doused the fire on this spot, but there was no sign left of any campsite.

"This is awfully close to the fire line," Walker observed. "Bad place to set up."

"Do you —" Rodgers began. His voice caught in his throat, and he had to start again. "Do you see any bodies?"

"No."

"Okay . . . So if they were here, that means they got out."

Walker nodded thoughtfully. "So where do you reckon they'd go? Back to their buggy?"

"They should. Do we know where it is?"

Walker tapped his smart watch to life and began flicking through apps on the touchscreen. He kept his eye on the projection screen in his goggles until he had the information he wanted. When he got it, he swiped the information he'd found from his smart watch toward Rodgers's datapad. Rodgers looked out the window vaguely in the direction of where the buggy should have been parked, but smoke made it impossible to see.

"This is where they should be going," Rodgers said to the pilot, holding up the datapad beside him. The pilot glanced at the map depicted on the small screen and pointed the helicopter in the right direction. The fire wasn't spreading that way yet, but it was only a matter of time.

As the helicopter drew closer, Walker finally spotted the Badgers' buggy parked at a scenic overlook with an old set of stairs leading down to an overgrown hiking trail. The aircraft's rotors tore the low-hanging smoke over the area to shreds as it descended to give the spotters a clearer view.

"I hope this isn't his escape route," Sergeant Rodgers said. "It's all uphill and overgrown. What are you thinking, Ethan?"

Walker said nothing, but Rodgers could

see the ranger shared his opinion. Escaping uphill from any danger was always a bad call. Trying to escape from a fire uphill was even worse. Wildfire traveled faster uphill.

"See anything?" the pilot called over his shoulder.

"There's nobody here," Rodgers said. "They must still be out in the woods."

"Maybe they're trying to dig new lines around the fire where it got out," Walker suggested.

"Without calling it in?" Rodgers asked. "And with their camp torched? No. Ethan knows better than that. He's trying to get his people back here. At least he'd better be . . ." He turned to the pilot. "Take us back over the canopy. We'll try to spot their trail in the middle somewhere."

"Heath . . ." Walker began.

"It's all right," Rodgers cut him off. "I

remember this area pretty well from when I was a kid. I know some places we can start looking to try to pick them up."

"Does your brother know the area as well as you do?"

Rodgers frowned. He held out a hand and tipped it side to side. "So-so. He didn't come out here as often." Walker's dubious expression did not fade. "It's all right, I've got an idea." He turned back to the pilot and laid that idea out. The pilot shrugged and guided the helicopter back the way they'd come.

The last leg of the flight was short, but it felt like an eternity to Rodgers. *Come on, Ethan*, he thought. *Where are you?*

CHAPTER SEVEN

"I warned you," the helicopter pilot told Sergeant Rodgers. "The fire's coming this way. You've got about an hour before this whole area's going to be too hot to stay in."

The search-and-rescue helicopter hovered over a clearing halfway between the Badgers' broken fire line and their buggy. The spot wasn't big enough for the helicopter to land, but it was enough to debark the search team.

As the aircraft hovered, it paid out two lengths of cable from over the doors on each side. Rodgers, Walker, and the rest of the search party clipped carabiners from rappelling harnesses onto those cables.

"We got it," Sergeant Rodgers told the pilot, shouting over the wind through the open door. "Just keep your eyes on the road, and tell us if they pop out."

The pilot gave a thumbs-up.

Sergeant Rodgers tossed him a quick salute then stepped backward out of the door to the runner, letting the cable take his weight. Beside him, Walker did the same.

With a nod to each other, they leaned out and fast-roped down the cables. Their boots touched ground in seconds. They unclipped, backed off and made room for the rest of the search team.

When everyone was down, Sergeant Rodgers gave the signal on his radio. The helicopter rose immediately, slurping the cables back up like spaghetti. The pilot wished him good luck, and he was off.

The search team consisted of eight people, including Sergeant Rodgers and Ranger Walker. The group's leader was a man ten years younger than Rodgers. When Rodgers stepped up, the man deferred to him.

"Okay, let's spread west," Sergeant Rodgers began. "These woods are full of old deer trails and overgrown logging paths impossible to see from the air. Ethan and his guys could be on any one of them. They've had plenty of time to get past us, so if you find a trail, follow it toward the road, not toward the fire. If you find a sign they've been on it, radio the rest of us. We'll start heading your way. Everybody got each other on GPS?"

The searchers all checked their smartphones and nodded.

"Let's move out."

Sergeant Rodgers and the others peeled off along the search line, putting the direction of the fire on their left. They quickly lost sight of one another in the thick timber and undergrowth, forcing them to rely on radio and GPS to stay in contact. Rodgers and Walker took the last leg, with Rodgers moving out to the farthest position.

When they were all in position, their search line drew a broad arc out in front of the fire line.

Years ago, Rodgers had hiked and camped in these woods, but today they barely resembled the forests of his youth. The fire made a difference, of course. The wind carried smoke in along the ground, making the place resemble some haunted moor. The trees had transformed into dried skeletons as the heat sucked the moisture out of them.

Even at this distance from the actual fire, its heat was oppressive in the muggy summer afternoon. The wind kicked up dirt and leaves and occasionally flicked around brightly glowing ember specks. The landscape was the same, but it was as if Rodgers were remembering it in the grip of a nightmare. The eerie blowing of the wind and the distant roar of the fire heightened that sensation.

As Sergeant Rodgers pushed ahead through the undergrowth, he made a few attempts to reach his brother. The only response he got back on the radio on the Badgers' frequency was static.

He tried Ethan's cell phone, but it went straight to voicemail. Firefighters weren't supposed to use their cell phones on an incident site, but most firemen who had them carried them in case they needed to make job-related calls. Ethan's was apparently off, and Rodgers didn't know anyone else on his crew.

In a moment of inspiration, he radioed the rest of the search team to see if anyone else did. They didn't, so Rodgers sent a request up the chain to Michael Farrant back at Incident Command to get a list of their cell numbers.

If he and the search team couldn't raise the Badgers by radio, maybe at least one of them would have better luck by phone. Reception was dodgy out here, but there was coverage. Farrant told Rodgers he'd get right on it and get back to them.

Before that inquiry yielded results, Sergeant Rodgers stumbled onto a path. It wasn't wide enough to be visible from the air, but it was wide enough for two people, shoulder to shoulder.

He pushed out of the brush screening it from one side and gave it a good hard look.

It ran east to west, parallel to the search line, and showed signs. The marks on the ground signaled that something heavy was being dragged.

Sergeant Rodgers followed the path a bit back toward Ranger Walker's direction and found confirmation that *someone* had been here: a fresh boot print in a patch of soft earth. It was the right size and shape of a logging boot just like the kind Rodgers and most of the other wildland firefighters wore.

The only thing was, it was facing west, heading outside the search perimeter. The way the path curved, it was moving away from the direction of the road and the buggy.

"This is Search One," Rodgers said to the rest of the team over the radio. "I've got something. Tracks leading west on a fresh path at my location. Anybody else see anything?"

A chorus of negatives came back.

Walker added, "West? You sure it's them, Sergeant?"

"Not a hundred percent," Sergeant Rodgers replied. "It's possible, though."

"Why would they be going west?"

"I don't know." Rodgers sighed. "It doesn't make sense. But nothing else about this makes any sense either."

"Should we form up on you?" the search-and-rescue leader asked.

"No," Rodgers said. "Keep up the sweep in case I'm reading this wrong. I'll play the path out a little while."

"We don't have much time," Walker pointed out. "Fire's coming."

Sergeant Rodgers checked the real-time fire map on his datapad. Walker was right, as if the ever-increasing roar of the fire behind him wasn't enough indication.

"I'll be quick. Just let me know if you guys find a better lead."

"Will do. And you likewise."

Sergeant Rodgers headed off down the path in the wrong direction. As he did, he hoped without hope that his little brother had had more sense than to do the same.

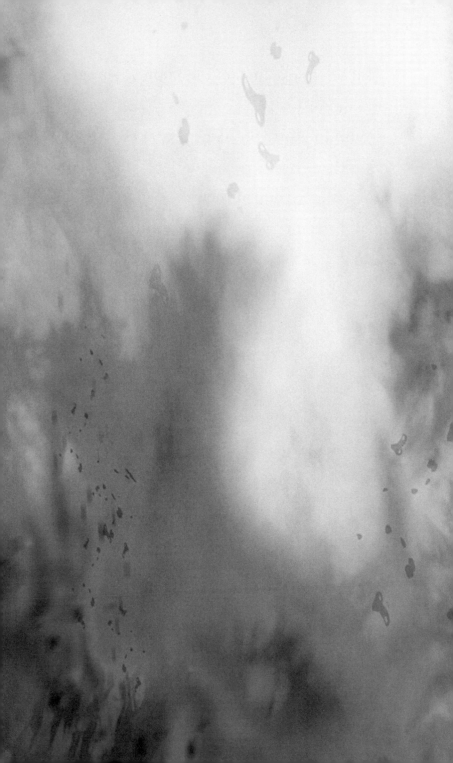

CHAPTER EIGHT

Nothing but static.

Then Sergeant Rodgers's two-way radio went silent. He looked at the radio's power light, which usually glowed green. It was black. Dead. Rodgers had no other way to communicate with the search-and-rescue chopper he'd just sent away. He had no way to evacuate — except on foot.

So Rodgers kept moving. Although he hadn't found any sign as strong as another boot print, evidence still suggested people had moved down this path in this direction as early as this morning.

Sergeant Rodgers pressed on past the twenty-minute mark and neared twenty-five. One by one, the other searchers began to report that they'd reached the road, all without finding anything. Even the chopper pilot had come up empty and added his voice to that of the others urging Rodgers to pull out and head north. Farrant had come through eventually with the Hotshots' personal cell numbers, but no one had been able to reach them.

As time ticked down, things were looking grim.

At the half-hour mark after finding the path, Rodgers had almost given up when he heard the faint hint of a sound up ahead. It was a pair of voices. He couldn't recognize them at this distance, but he didn't have to.

With new hope swelling, Rodgers took off at a run.

Rounding a bend, Rodgers broke into a shadowy glade where ten sweaty, tired men and women were arguing with a figure in the center. As one, they stopped when Rodgers appeared.

"What the heck are you doing here?" the figure in the center of the group demanded.

It was Ethan.

"I'm looking for you!" Rodgers snapped back. "Why aren't you answering your radio?"

Ethan shook his head and slapped the radio holstered on his belt. "We can't get a signal out."

"What about your phones? I've been trying to call you for an hour. All of you guys."

"They're at camp," one of the other Hotshots said, glaring at Ethan, his flailing leader.

"Your camp's gone," Rodgers reported. "What happened?"

Ethan shook his head and sighed. Rodgers had never seen him look so exhausted and weak. A part of him wanted to just scoop him up and hug him right there in front of everybody. He somehow doubted that would have been especially helpful.

"We had a spot fire," Ethan said. "It blew up — fast. By the time we had everybody up and out of harm's way, we couldn't get a line around it fast enough to contain it."

"Okay, I get why you didn't call that in, but why didn't you go back to your buggy?"

"What do you think we're trying to do?" Ethan replied hotly.

"This isn't the way there."

"Yeah, look, the fire cut us off from our escape route, so we were heading to Flatt Ridge to get back onto the road."

"Flatt Ridge?" Rodgers asked, puzzled. "That's five miles back in the other direction."

"I told you we were going the wrong way!" the Hotshot who'd spoken earlier crowed.

Rodgers and Ethan both whipped a glare of death at him and barked, "Shut up!"

He did.

Rodgers brought up a map on his datapad and showed it to Ethan. "Look, *this* is where we are. Here's your campsite. Here's the road where your buggy's parked. *This* is Flatt Ridge."

Ethan went pale. "But I thought . . . I mean . . . We hiked on this path before. I remember it."

Rodgers shook his head, feeling his brother's pain and confusion in his own guts. "Not this path, man. This wasn't here when we were kids. I don't know where this even goes."

Ethan wavered slightly on his feet as the enormity of his mistake sank in. He looked up at Rodgers, and for a moment all Rodgers could see was the little seven-year-old kid who'd broken Dad's car windshield with a baseball.

"What do we —"A tremendous explosive *CRACK!* cut off Ethan's question. Rodgers flinched, remembering too many bad times in the Marines. It took him a second to realize what had happened. As the fire drew closer, it was heating up the sap in the trees in its path. That sap bubbled and boiled in its veins, and when it couldn't get out of the tree fast enough, it simply tore the tree apart from the inside. Before Rodgers could even process that realization, another tree exploded somewhere back along the path. A hot wind stirred the smoke and underbrush around them, carrying flakes of ash.

"We need to move," Sergeant Rodgers ordered. "That fire's right on top of us." He checked the real-time fire map for confirmation. A finger of the fire had raced out ahead of the rest and now lay across the path back the way he'd come. They couldn't go back that way. He told Ethan.

"We'll just have to cut north," Ethan said. "Straight overland, back to the road."

"Look," Rodgers said, showing him the map. "We can't go that way. It's all uphill from here, and it gets too steep just before the road. If this wind keeps up, it's going to blow the fire right on top of us up there. We're going to have to go around to the northwest here."

"We can't get back to the road that way," Ethan said.

"No, but look, there's a big meadow down on this side. It's big enough for a helicopter." Rodgers grabbed the two-way radio on his belt. "Oh . . . right," he muttered to himself.

"There's no sense waiting here," Sergeant Rodgers told Ethan and the other Hotshots. They looked to him for leadership now, which earned him a glare from Ethan. "Let's go."

Rodgers headed out at a brisk jog, pushing back into the underbrush. It was hard going, but the rising smoke and heat forced them onward.

The Badgers were tough, as all Hotshots must be, so they made good time away from the fire front. None of them complained about the pace, despite a whole day of wandering. They forced their way through the trackless woods, winding around the steep hills that stood in their way.

Eventually, the trees thinned out and gave way to tall grass and high weeds. The firefighters emerged into the sunlight and took in the view. The meadow wasn't quite as big as it had seemed on Rodgers's map. Bordered by a steep rocky ridge on the far side, a dry streambed to the east, and trees to the west and south, it wasn't much bigger than half a football field. It was open, sure, and wide enough for choppers, but it wasn't much protection from the oncoming fire.

"What now, Heath?" Ethan said, peering over his shoulder.

"We wait," Rodgers replied.

"For what?!" Ethan exclaimed. "We don't have any way to communicate with search and rescue."

"That doesn't mean they don't know we're here," said Rodgers. He placed a firm hand on his brother's shoulder. "When one thing breaks, you don't give up on everything else."

Other Hotshots looked on in awkward silence.

"Ahem!" Rodgers cleared his throat and

released his grip on Ethan's shoulder. "I mean, trust the system, kid. It's there for a reason."

"Well, the fire's getting awfully close."

"We'll be okay," Rodgers assured him. It didn't have the comforting ring of older-brother authority Ian's voice would have had.

Ethan sighed and looked at his Hotshots. They huddled together in the grass to rest. None of them seemed eager to meet Ethan's gaze.

"This is all my fault," he said softly. "I screwed this up pretty bad."

"You made some bad calls," Sergeant Rodgers said. "You set your camp —"

"Too close to the fire. I know."

"Your escape route to your buggy's a shambles. Plus you let yourself get turned around."

"This is a bad pep talk," Ethan said.

Sergeant Rodgers gave him a wry smile.

"This isn't all on you," he allowed. "If your guys had better gear, you wouldn't have had so many problems. At the very least, we could have gotten to you last night when you needed help."

"I guess." He sighed again and sat down on the ground. Rodgers squatted beside him. "Looks like you were right. I wouldn't have made a very good Firestormer. Your chief told me you said so. Thanks for that, by the way."

Rodgers closed his eyes. *Now* Ethan wanted to talk about this? "Look, Ethan —"

"No," Ethan said. "You were right. I've been salty about it for a while, but I don't have much room to argue with you anymore, do I?"

"Listen, you've still got plenty of career left to come back from this," Rodgers said. "This isn't even all that bad. You got a little lost, but you didn't get anybody killed. And you got your fire lines dug faster than anybody I've ever seen. If it weren't for some spots of bad luck, you guys would have the whole thing locked down by now."

"Bad luck, huh?"

Rodgers scoffed. "That's just the nature of the work, man. These fires are like . . . Well, they're like William's kids."

"Huh?"

"They don't do what they're supposed to no matter how much you tell them to."

Ethan chuckled, though a little guiltily.

"You're not the only guy who's ever made a mistake in the field," Rodgers said. "All you can do is learn from it and do better next time. And count your blessings it wasn't worse."

Ethan cocked an eyebrow. "That almost sounds like experience."

"It is," Rodgers admitted. "Just not

firefighting experience. Remember how I never tell anybody why I left the Corps? It's that kind of experience."

"Oh. You want to talk about it?"

"It's classified. I could tell you, but then I'd have to kill you."

Ethan huffed. "Jerk."

Rodgers grinned.

"Listen!" Ethan observed as the sound of helicopter rotors thumped in the distance.

"Told you," Rodgers said. "That's our ride."

"What do you suppose Command's going to do with us now?"

"I'm taking you guys back to my camp," Rodgers told him. "I'm sure my lieutenant's going to shuffle your guys in with mine for the time being. He'll divide up and redeploy us. Some of us will work on our lines up north while the rest of us dig out new ones to get your fire back under control."

"Oh," Ethan said. "I just thought . . ."

"What? Did you think you were going to get benched just because of a little setback? Sorry, kiddo. The fight goes on. At least this way we get to fight it together for a while."

"I guess so," Ethan said. He looked up as the rescue helicopter came into view and began its slow descent. "And, Heath, one more thing before I forget . . ."

"Yeah?"

"The next time your boss asks you if I'm qualified for a job, keep your fat stupid trap shut."

Rodgers smirked. "No guarantees."

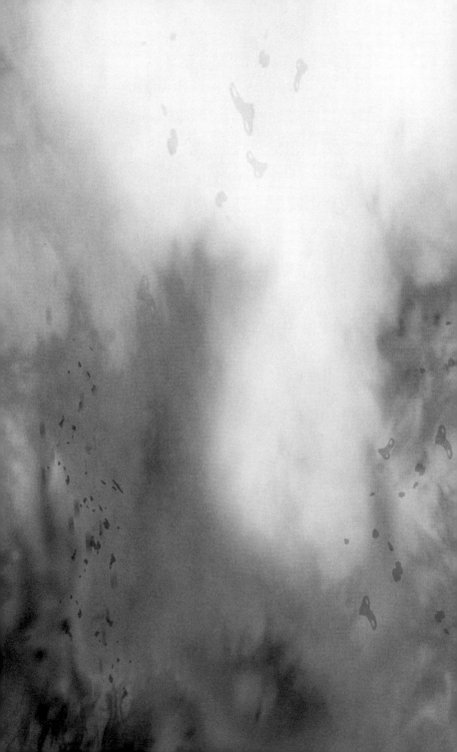

ABOUT THE AUTHOR

Carl Bowen is a father, husband, and writer living in Lawrenceville, Georgia. He has published a handful of novels, short stories, and comics. For Stone Arch Books and Capstone, Carl has retold *20,000 Leagues Under the Sea* (by Jules Verne), *The Strange Case of Dr. Jekyll and Mr. Hyde* (by Robert Louis Stevenson), *The Jungle Book* (by Rudyard Kipling), "Aladdin and His Wonderful Lamp" (from *A Thousand and One Nights*), *Julius Caesar* (by William Shakespeare), and *The Murders in the Rue Morgue* (by Edgar Allan Poe). Carl's novel, *Shadow Squadron: Elite Infantry*, earned a starred review from *Kirkus Book Reviews*.

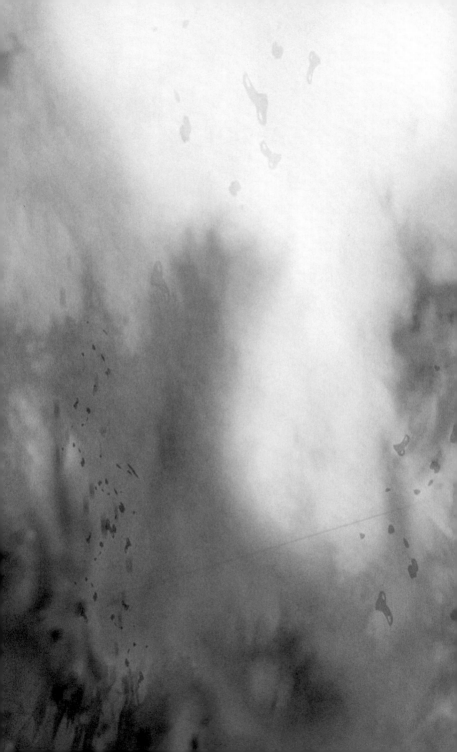

GLOSSARY

fire marshal (FIRE MAR-shul) — a member of the fire department whose duties include enforcing fire codes and investigating fire origins and causes

Hotshot (HOT-shot) — a member of handcrew of firefighters that are specially trained in wildfire suppression tactics

isolated (eye-suh-LAY-tudh) — all alone

jurisdiction (jur-uhs-DIK-shuhn) — legal power to interpret and administer the law in a specific area

orienteering (or-ee-uhn-TIHR-ing) — a skill in which people have to find their way across rough using a map and compass

perimeter (puh-RIM-uh-tur) — the outer edge or boundary of an area

terrain (tuh-RAYN) — the surface of the land

FIREFIGHTING EQUIPMENT

PULASKI AXE
A single-bit ax with an adze-shaped
hoe extending from the back.

MCLEOD
A combination hoe and rake used especially
by the U.S. Forest Service in firefighting.

CHAIN SAW
A tool that cuts wood with a circular chain that is driven
by a motor and made up of many connected sharp metal
teeth. Sawyers use chain saws to fell trees on the fire line.

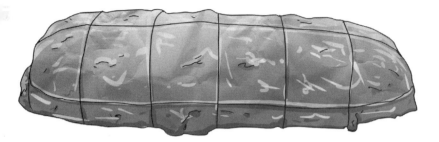

FIRE SHELTER
A small, aluminized tent offering protection in an emergency. The shelter reflect radiant heat and provides breathable air if a firefighter becomes trapped within a blaze.

DRIPTORCH
A handheld canister containing flammable fuel. When ignited, firefighters use driptorches to "drip" flames onto the ground for a controlled burn.

TWO-WAY RADIO
A small radio for receiving and sending messages.

WILDFIRE FACTS

Nearly 90% of wildfires are started by humans. Most of these fires begin by accidental causes, including careless campfires and poorly discarded cigarettes.

Lightning is the leading cause of natural wildfires. Every day, lightning strikes the Earth more than 100,000 times, and 10–20% of those strikes ignite a fire. However, most lightning fires are small and burn out quickly.

An average of 1.2 million acres of forest burns in the United States every year. In 2015, more than 10 million acres burned, setting a new record. Battling these fires costs $1.7 billion.

In extreme wildfires, flames can tower more than 165 feet in the air and reach temperatures of 2,200 degrees Fahrenheit.

The Great Miramichi Fire is the largest wildfire ever recorded. The blaze burned more than 3 million acres throughout New Brunswick, Canada, and Maine, in October 1825. During the fire, 160 lives were lost.

On June 30, 2013, nineteen members of the Granite City Hotshots were killed during the Yarnell Hill Fire in Yarnell, Arizona. It was the deadliest day for U.S. firefighters since the terrorist attacks on September 11, 2001.

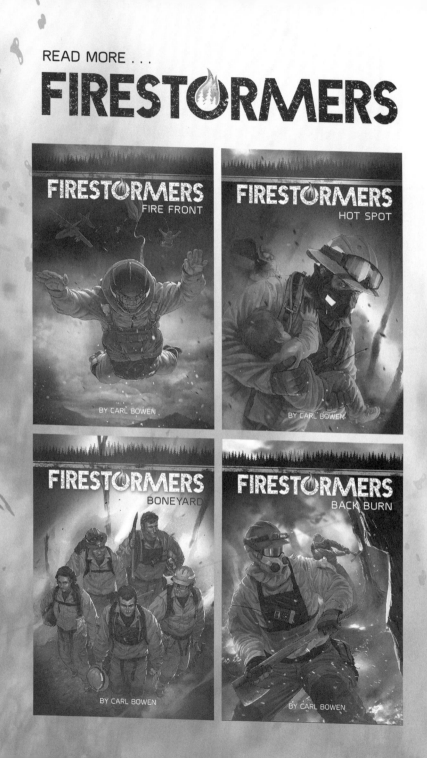

THEN CHECK OUT . . .
SHADOW SQUADRON
ALSO BY CARL BOWEN

ONLY FROM STONE ARCH BOOKS

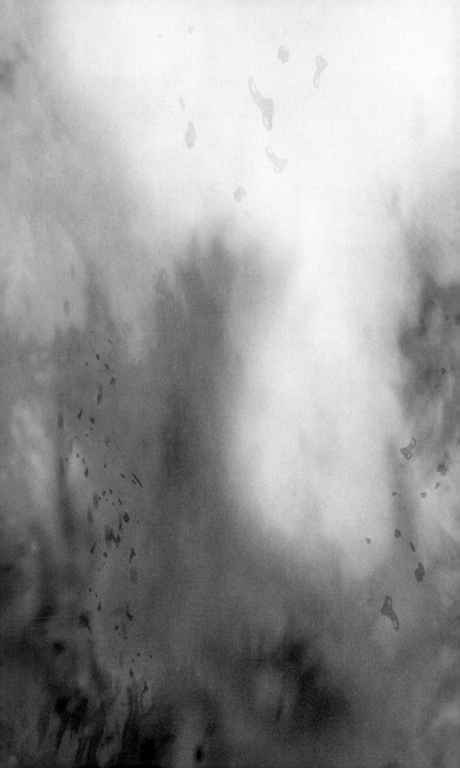